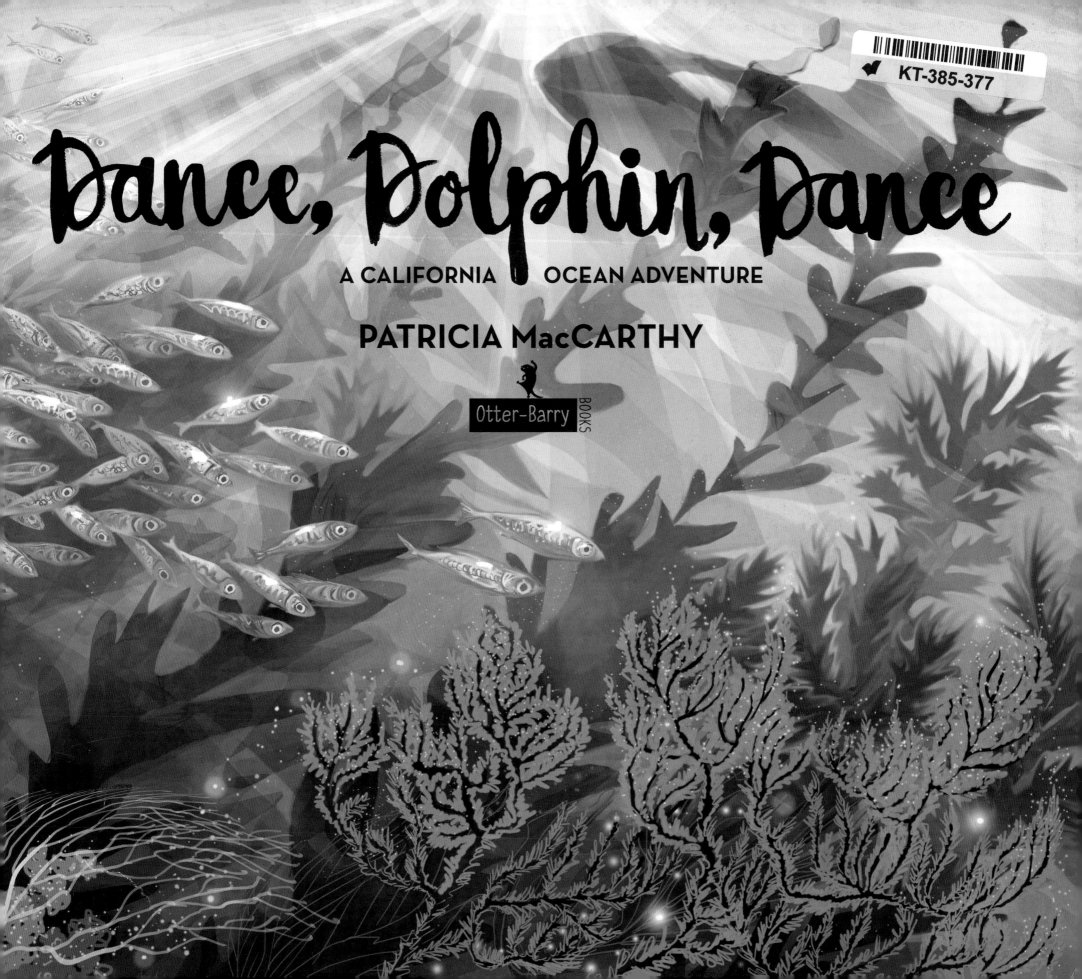

Dance, Dolphin, Dance

A CALIFORNIA OCEAN ADVENTURE

PATRICIA MacCARTHY

Otter-Barry BOOKS

Out in the ocean the sea is surging,
swishswosh, **swishswosh**
and deep down below,
the kelp forest gently sways.

A shoal of sardines
swirls and shimmers, swirls and shimmers.
Playful Dolphin dances with them.

The sea softly rocks
back and *forth*, back and *forth*

while towers of kelp
ripple and tug, ripple and tug.

Now sea lions join in
Dolphin's dance.

The water is getting rough.
whoosh swoosh whoosh swoosh
and the giant kelp
twirls and twists, twirls and twists.
Creatures are coming into the
seaweed forest to shelter from
the choppy sea outside.

Some sparkly tuna join in Dolphin's dance,
tossing and turning, tossing and turning.

The rough sea **rolls and tumbles, rolls and tumbles,**
ripping and pulling at the kelp.

A **BIG** Blue Whale
glides past and
blocks Dolphin's
dance.

But Dolphin **loops up and over** the Blue Whale's back,

straight into ...

a Great WHITE **SHARK**!

Whoosh! The shark attacks,
but Dolphin is faster.
With a **PUFF of bubbles**,
he leaps away from
those great, white,
gnashing teeth.

Dance,
Dolphin, dance.
Dance for your life!

The chase is on!

Quick and nimble, Dolphin **loops and hΟΟps, loops and hΟΟps,** and dashes down to the deepest part of the kelp forest.

But he can't hide there,
for a KILLER WHALE is **lurking** in the shadows.

Now Dolphin is being hunted by
a Great WHITE **SHARK** and
a KILLER WHALE!

zig zag zig zag
Dolphin dances for
his life in the deep,
dark kelp forest.

Dolphin struggles up to
the surface of the ocean.
splOsh splash splOsh splash
But it is rough and wild, and huge waves
Crash and drag, Crash and drag.

BANG! A powerful wave hits the
Great WHITE **SHARK** and the KILLER WHALE.
boom-boom boom-boom

They roll and collide.
Then they turn on each other.
Dolphin slips silently away – and escapes.

Back at the kelp forest,
Dolphin finds his
friends and they

dip and dive, dip and dive,
until the sea is calm again.

Then, as the sun sets,
up they swim to play with the seabirds.
flip flash, flip flash
Dolphin is safe at last, and together
all the dolphins dance for joy.

Can you find these 36 sea creatures and birds in the book?
They all live in and around the California kelp forest
in the Pacific Ocean.

Great Blue Heron

Manta Ray

Leatherback Sea Turtle

Brown Rockfish

Spotted Sharpnose Puffer

Pacific Bluefin Tuna

Great White Shark

Bat Star

Moon Jelly

Whale Shark

Pacific Sardine

Garibaldi

Yellowtail Surgeonfish

Bottlenose Dolphin

East Pacific Red Octopus

Flag Rockfish

Blue Whale

Brown Pelican

California Sea Lion

California
Least Tern

Juvenile King
Angelfish

Cortez
Bonefish

California Sheephead

Indo-
Pacific Sailfish

Killer
Whale

Longnose Hawkfish

Crowned
Squirrelfish

Blue-footed
Booby

Cortez
Angelfish

Cannonball
Jellyfish

Panamic
Soldierfish

Grouper

Bluestriped
Grunt

Sea
Otter

Hammerhead Shark

Green Sea Turtle